The Oyster's Journey

Written by Kirsty Holmes

Illustrated by Brandon Mattless

It is Dad's birthday today. I am on holiday with Mum and Dad, my brother Lloyd and my baby sister, Lucy-May. Dad loves to sail, so we are here at Coyne Bay to go on a trip on a sailing ship!

THIS DIARY BELONGS TO:

Taylor Joyce

Aged 7 3/4

The Oyster's Journey

©Published 2022.
BookLife Publishing Ltd.
King's Lynn, Norfolk PE30 4LS

ISBN 978-1-80155-167-0

The Oyster's Journey
Written by Kirsty Holmes
Illustrated by Brandon Mattless

An Introduction to Accessible Readers...

Our 'really readable' Accessible Readers have been specifically created to support the reading development of young readers with learning differences, such as dyslexia.

Our aim is to share our love of books with children, providing the same learning and developmental opportunities to every child.

INCREASED FONT SIZE AND SPACING improves readability and ensures text feels much less crowded.

OFF-WHITE BACKGROUNDS ON MATTE PAPER improves text contrast and avoids dazzling readers.

SIMPLIFIED PAGE LAYOUT reduces distractions and aids concentration.

CAREFULLY CRAFTED along guidelines set out in the British Dyslexia Association's Dyslexia-Friendly Style Guide.

It is windy at Coyne Bay, but Dad says we can go sailing anyway. He says it will be more fun that way! We are staying in a guest house called The Royal Maypole. Our room is small and bright.

THE ROYAL MAYPOLE GUEST HOUSE

This morning we met Captain Joy. Captain Joy is big and jolly. Her ship, the Oyster, is a sailing boat. She says the Oyster is called the Oyster because she's a real pearl. Captain Joy says we all have to listen to her and do what she says.

Captain Joy steered the ship until we were out of Coyne Bay. It was strange watching the land slowly move away, but it was exciting, so it was okay. My hair was damp from the sea spray. Now Mum is putting our stuff away.

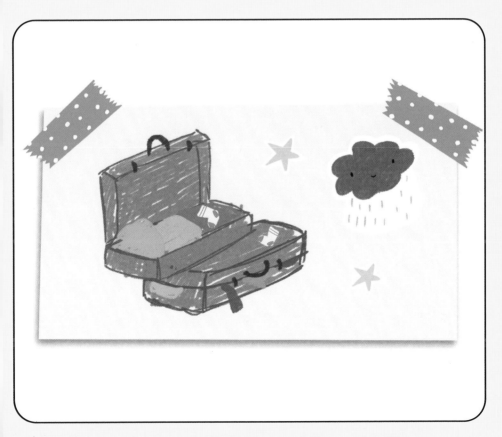

Captain Joy told us a story tonight...
Captain Joy says Big Wayne is the
biggest whale ever, and that he lives
in the seas around Coyne Bay! I want
to see him, but she says only pirates
get to see Big Wayne.

Big Wayne

There are books next to my bed. I found one called 'Far, Far Away'. It is all about how sailors find their way using the stars. Lloyd is reading it while I write this. The Oyster rocks and sways at night. It makes me sleepy...

This morning when we got up, Captain Joy was not as joyful as yesterday. She said there were grey clouds over Coyne Bay, and we should have a short trip. We set out across the bay. All of a sudden, it got dark.

"Lloyd, take Lucy-May and Taylor downstairs please," said Dad, as salty sea spray crashed up the side of the Oyster. "The storm is coming in fast."

Lloyd took Lucy-May downstairs where it was safer.

The Oyster was swaying from side to side through the storm. Lloyd said we had turned away from the bay and were heading out to sea!

"It'll be okay," he said. "Don't cry, Lucy-May. Captain Joy will keep us safe."

When the Oyster stopped swaying, we headed up to the top deck.

"Where is Coyne Bay?" I asked. It had disappeared.

"We don't know," said Dad. "The storm swept us away."

"The Oyster is not a sea vessel," said Captain Joy. "She never leaves the bay. I don't have anything to find our way."

Suddenly, I remembered. 'Far, Far Away'! I ran to grab the book and gave it to Dad.

"Maybe we can find our way back to the bay the old-fashioned way!" I said. "We can let the stars light our way!"

"Clever Taylor," said Dad.

"Hooray!" said Captain Joy.

This afternoon we saw a group of huge manta rays! They were so playful! They swam around the Oyster for a while, and for a moment we all forgot we were lost and far away from the bay. Then they disappeared.

"Where did they go?" asked Lloyd.

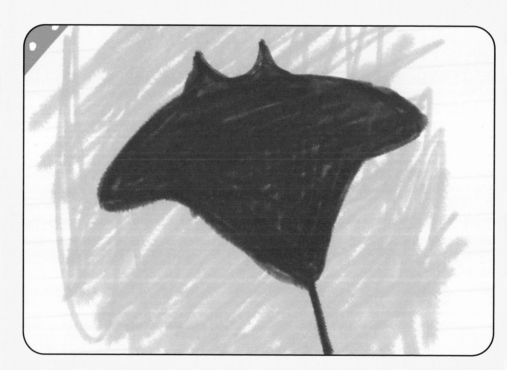

They just suddenly went away! Captain Joy said something must have made them swim away. I wonder what it could be... Captain Joy thinks she knows the way to land. She says watching the Sun can tell you which way to go, too.

Later on, I asked Captain Joy if we might see Big Wayne out at sea. She smiled at me, and then she told me about her grandmother, Captain Caraway Joy.

"She saw it once, Taylor," said Captain Joy.

Captain Caraway Joy.

"Big Wayne."

Just then, the Oyster gave a shudder.

"What was that?" asked Dad. There was a long pause. Then there was a long, low sound. Something was bumping the Oyster... from below!

I looked at Captain Joy in dismay.

"Is it... Big Wayne?" I asked.

"Hold on tight!" said Dad.

I grabbed Captain Joy, who held on to Lucy-May. Lloyd, Mum and Dad grabbed the mast, and we held on to the wheel.

Then, suddenly, the Oyster flew into the air!

"Hooray!" said Lucy-May.

"We're going to be destroyed!" shouted Lloyd.

"Not while I'm Captain!" boomed Captain Joy. "Is everyone okay?" called Dad.

It was Big Wayne!

There was another low, rumbling sound. The whale was so big that the sound made the Oyster rock and sway.

"Hang on!" cried Mum. "Is he trying to say something?"

Mum reached over and grabbed the picnic basket, then threw it over the side!

"I think he's trying to say he's hungry!" she said.

"Poor boy." Thank goodness Mum brought enough food for a voyage! We threw it all to Big Wayne.

Big Wayne ate all our cakes and sandwiches. Then he slowly slipped away into the inky-black sea.

"Wayne gone away," said Lucy-May.

"Bye Wayne." Lucy-May waved to Wayne. Big Wayne gave a huge, playful flick of his giant tail.

"Hold on!" shouted Mum. "It looks like we're going to ride a wave!"

Big Wayne's tail had made a huge wave. It pushed the Oyster up and along. It felt like being on a rollercoaster. Soon, we were bobbing in calm water again.

"Hooray!" we all cried.

"Look!" shouted Lloyd. "LAND AHOY!"

"It is, my boy!" cried Captain Joy, looking through her telescope.

"Land ahoy indeed!" And we all jumped with joy.

The Oyster had landed ashore in a place called Runaway Bay. Everyone wanted to know how we had crossed the whole sea in the Oyster!

"It was meant to be a day trip," said Dad. "We only made it this far thanks to a book."

"We didn't mean to go on a voyage!"

Captain Joy was enjoying telling the tale of 'Big Wayne and the Accidental Voyage' so much that she even got to go on television!

"And it was all thanks to Big Wayne," she said.

Having my photo in the newspaper was okay, but all I really wanted was to go sailing again.

"Can we go again, Dad?" I asked.

"Maybe," said Dad. "But now it's time for a different holiday..."

The Oyster's Journey: Quiz

1. What was the weather like at Coyne Bay?

2. Why were the family at Coyne Bay?

3. How did Taylor describe Captain Joy?

4. Why did Lloyd have to take Lucy-May and Taylor to the downstairs of the boat?

5. How would you have felt if you were aboard the Oyster? Would you want to go sailing again?

Helpful Hints for Reading at Home

This 'really readable' Accessible Reader has been carefully written and designed to help children with learning differences whether they are reading in the classroom or at home. However, there are some extra ways in which you can help your child at home.

- Try to provide a quiet space for your child to read, with as few distractions as possible.

- Try to allow your child as much time as they need to decode the letters and words on the page.

- Reading with a learning difference can be frustrating and difficult. Try to let your child take short, managed breaks between reading sessions if they begin to feel frustrated.

- Build your child's confidence with positive praise and encouragement throughout.

- Your child's teacher, as well as many charities, can provide you with lots of tips and techniques to help your child read at home.